Raffle Ticket No 7
10p
Woodside Dry Cleaners. receipt for Jacket and bow tie.
Mouse
STAMFORD, LINCS.
Dear Mouse,
Weather fine and sunny. Have been picnicing on common. Love Rat.
Mr. Mouse The woods (Just past Rabbits hole)

SCUNTHORPE-ON-SEA
Having a lovely time, wish you were here! from Rabbit
To Mole esq.
The Woods
(Near Owls tree)
(Don't know Postcode)
Mole
you are cordially invited to Rabbits birthday party.
Bring a cake. R.S.V.P.
your sight
To be kept
MoLe

For dear old Frog and Toad

献给亲爱的青蛙和蟾蜍

中英双语

老鼠和鼹鼠

和你聊天真好呀

[英]乔伊斯·邓巴 著 [英]詹姆斯·梅修 绘 仇春卉 译

中信出版集团 | 北京

图书在版编目（CIP）数据

老鼠和鼹鼠. 和你聊天真好呀 / (英) 乔伊斯・邓巴著 ; (英) 詹姆斯・梅修绘 ; 仇春卉译. -- 北京 : 中信出版社, 2021.10（2025. 4重印）
ISBN 978-7-5217-3409-6

Ⅰ. ①老… Ⅱ. ①乔… ②詹… ③仇… Ⅲ. ①儿童故事-图画故事-英国-现代 Ⅳ. ①I561.85

中国版本图书馆CIP数据核字(2021)第151276号

老鼠和鼹鼠・和你聊天真好呀

著　　者：［英］乔伊斯・邓巴
绘　　者：［英］詹姆斯・梅修
译　　者：仇春卉
出版发行：中信出版集团股份有限公司
（北京市朝阳区东三环北路27号嘉铭中心　邮编　100020）
承 印 者：北京启航东方印刷有限公司

开　　本：889mm × 1194mm　1/16　　印　　张：3.25　　字　　数：60 千字
版　　次：2021 年 10 月第 1 版　　印　　次：2025 年 4 月第 9 次印刷
京权图字：01-2021-1891
书　　号：ISBN 978-7-5217-3409-6
定　　价：28.00元

出　　品：中信儿童书店
图书策划：如果童书
策划编辑：安虹　　责任编辑：孙婧媛　安虹　　营销编辑：张远　邝青青　张超
封面设计：谢佳静　　内文排版：王莹

目录

和我聊天吧

“和我聊天吧。”老鼠说。

“聊什么呢？”鼹鼠说。

“聊什么都行。”老鼠说。

“我什么也想不出来，”鼹鼠说，“给我出点儿主意嘛。”

“你可以问问我，明天我们打算做什么。”老鼠说。

“那明天我们打算做什么呢？”鼹鼠说。

“这个嘛，”老鼠说，“如果明天天气好，我们就去树林里野餐。我们要做些奶酪黄瓜三明治，还要带上新的野餐篮，篮子里放上茶杯、茶杯托，还有盘子。”

“好哇。”鼹鼠说，“可如果天气不好呢？”

“天气不好的话，”老鼠说，“我们就用苹果木柴在壁炉里生起火，然后舒舒服服地坐在扶手沙发里，一边烘栗子，一边烤马芬蛋糕，一边喝热巧克力。”

“好啊。”鼹鼠说，“那如果天气不好也不坏呢？”

“我们既不野餐也不生火。”老鼠说，“就收拾收拾屋子。”

“就这么办。”鼹鼠说。

“谢谢你和我聊天。”老鼠说。

“别客气。”鼹鼠说。

沙拉

鼹鼠的大鼻子从被子里伸了出来。

“今天天气怎么样？”他问。

“狂风暴雨，又湿又冷。”老鼠说。

鼹鼠把大鼻子缩了回去。“这样的话，我还是躲在被窝里吧。”

“别担心，”老鼠说，“我会用苹果木柴在客厅里生起炉火，到时候你就愿意起床了。”

老鼠生起火，苹果木柴的烟味儿钻进鼹鼠的大鼻子里。过了一小会儿，他就拖着懒洋洋的身子下楼了。

“我最讨厌狂风暴雨、又湿又冷的日子。”他抱怨说，“我们什么也干不了，只能烤烤火。”

“我们还能干些别的。”老鼠说，“比如烤马芬蛋糕，烘栗子。”

“好啊，”鼹鼠说，“我还真是饿了。”

于是，老鼠烤了一些马芬蛋糕，又烘了一些栗子。

鼹鼠吃完整整一盘马芬蛋糕，马上问：“还有吗？”

鼹鼠吃完第二盘马芬蛋糕，又问：“还有吗？”

“我吃得太多啦。”鼹鼠吃光第三盘马芬蛋糕，然后说，“明天我只吃沙拉。”

“好主意。”老鼠说。

“确实是个好主意。”鼹鼠说，“既然这样，为什么要等到明天呢？健康饮食，马上开始。老鼠，我们有沙拉吗？”

“有。”老鼠说，“我们有胡萝卜、小萝卜和菠菜。”

“那就各来一点儿吧。”鼹鼠说，结果他吃了满满一盘沙拉。

“我表现够好吧？”他说，“我把沙拉全吃光了，真应该得到一点儿奖励。老鼠，给那些马芬蛋糕抹上黄油，再烘些栗子吧。”

最后，鼹鼠又吃了满满的一大盘。“原来又湿又冷的日子也不算太糟糕。”说完，他就打起了盹儿。

收拾屋子

“太好啦！”第二天早上，老鼠说，“今天阳光灿烂，我们可以出去野餐了。”

“不行啊。”鼹鼠说，“我昨天吃撑了，我先吃了一些烤马芬蛋糕和沙拉，后来又吃了好多烤马芬蛋糕。今天我什么也不想吃，就想锻炼身体。”

鼹鼠走进客厅要锻炼身体时，却发现那里乱七八糟的。

“老鼠啊，我们得收拾一下客厅，好腾出地方让我做健身操。”

于是，老鼠弯腰把地板上的杂物都捡起来，鼹鼠收拾了架子上的小物品。然后，老鼠又把沙发上的零零碎碎都清理干净。最后，他们将所有杂物都搬进厨房里堆好。

“好啦！”完工后，老鼠说，“现在有地方给你做健身操啦！”

“那我的深呼吸训练怎么办？”鼹鼠说，“我需要清新的空气来深呼吸。老鼠，这里灰尘太多了，还得扫地除尘呢。”

于是，老鼠四爪着地，趴着清扫地板；鼹鼠踮起脚，拂去天花板和架子上的蜘蛛网。他们干得太卖力，不一会儿就累得上气不接下气了。

“哎哟！”大功告成后，老鼠气喘吁吁地说，“可把我累坏了，现在你总算能锻炼身体了吧？”

“锻炼身体！”鼹鼠说，“我也累坏了，还怎么锻炼？我现在需要喝一杯热茶。来吧，老鼠，跟我进厨房。我们应该沏一壶茶，好好慰劳一下自己。”

他俩走进厨房去沏茶，却发现这里乱七八糟的。

“老鼠啊，”鼹鼠说，“我们得收拾收拾厨房，要不连沏茶的地方也没有。”

于是，他们齐心合力收拾厨房，把一切零碎杂物都捡起来，又把所有小物品都收起来，全部堆进了卧室里。好不容易忙活完，白天已经溜走了。

“好啦！”完工后，鼹鼠说，“我们先整理了客厅，又收拾了厨房。现在不仅要喝杯热茶，还应该吃点儿东西慰劳一下自己。来点儿薄煎饼和糖浆如何？”

于是，老鼠煎了一叠薄饼，鼹鼠打开了一罐糖浆。

“我吃完得早点儿睡。”鼹鼠吃饱喝足了，说道。

“我也是。”老鼠说。

他们走进卧室，本想睡个早觉，却发现里面乱七八糟的。

“老鼠，”鼹鼠说，“你看看我的床，上面堆满了杂物。”

“你也看看我的床。”老鼠说，“上面放满了小零碎。”

可他们实在太累了，不管三七二十一，倒在床上呼呼大睡……

杂物

“救命啊！”第二天一早，鼹鼠就大声嚷嚷起来，“我被活埋了！”

“咱俩同病相怜呀。”老鼠说，“来吧，我们还得继续收拾呢。”

“可是我们昨天已经收拾过了。”鼹鼠说。

“昨天是收拾过了，可是收拾的方法不对。”老鼠说，“你得明白，问题出在这些杂物上：我们的杂物太多了。昨天谈不上是真正收拾屋子，只是把杂物从一个房间搬到另一个房间。今天得把它们都扔掉！”

“可我喜欢杂物。”鼹鼠说，“你不觉得杂七杂八的东西挺有趣吗？说不定哪天会派上用场呢。”

“留下杂物，或者腾出地方，”老鼠说，“你只能选一个。”

“可如果没有了杂物，腾出的地方用来放什么呢？”鼹鼠问。

“杂物是杂物，地方是地方，”老鼠说，“两者不能混为一谈呀。来吧，我们把一些杂物扔到垃圾站，好歹先腾出点儿地方。鼹鼠，帮我把那几个垃圾袋都装满吧。”

他们一起装满了三个垃圾袋。

“你是对的，老鼠。”装完了，鼹鼠说，“看看我们腾出来的地方，多么舒服啊！再也没有乱七八糟的杂物，再也不用收拾啦！”

“我们可以开摩托车运走这几个大袋子。”老鼠说，“这次谁来开？”

“和上次一样，”鼹鼠说，“我开。”

垃圾站里立着三个巨大的垃圾箱，一个写着“玻璃”，一个写着“纸张”，还有一个写着“金属”。

老鼠把报纸全都扔进写着“纸张”的垃圾箱里。“第一袋搞定！”他说。

“你快看看，那里有一堆漫画书呀。”鼹鼠说，“看起来挺有趣的，我一定要拿回家。”

于是，他装了满满一袋旧漫画书。

然后，老鼠把空的玻璃瓶罐都扔进写着“玻璃”的垃圾箱里。“又一袋搞定！”他说。

“你快看看那面旧镜子，”鼹鼠说，“还有那个鱼缸。我一定要拿回家，说不定哪天有用呢。”

于是，他把镜子和鱼缸都装进了另一个袋子里。

最后，老鼠把金属瓶罐都扔进写着“金属”的垃圾箱里。“最后一袋搞定！”他说。

“你快看看那些衣架、那个古董铁皮箱，还有那堆金属弹簧。我一定要拿回家，说不定哪天能派上用场呢。”

于是，他把最后一个垃圾袋也装满了。

鼹鼠和老鼠装了满满三大袋杂物，开着摩托车回家去。

“你真是英明呀，能提前想到要腾出那么多地方。”鼹鼠说，“现在就有地方摆放这些杂物了。”

鼹鼠把一袋子漫画书全部倒在沙发上，把鱼缸和镜子摆在架子上，把衣架、金属弹簧，还有铁皮箱子一股脑儿扔在地板上。这下子，老鼠和鼹鼠连下脚的地方都没了。

老鼠抓了抓脑袋。

“我说过了，你要么留下杂物，要么腾出地方，只能选一个，不能两个都占着啊。现在可好，我们只能待在外面了。”

老鼠郁闷地坐在门前的台阶上，鼹鼠拨弄着一根坏了的弹簧。“这是我特意带给你的。”鼹鼠说。

可是老鼠不高兴，一点也高兴不起来！

野餐

“我觉得今天可以去野餐，”老鼠说，“我好想出去好好走一走。”

“我也是。”鼹鼠说，“那天气怎么样？”

“挺好的。”老鼠说，“阳光灿烂，万里无云。”

“这样的话，我就该穿上T恤和短裤，戴上遮阳帽。”鼹鼠说。

“我来装野餐篮吧。”老鼠说。

他们很快就准备好出发了。刚刚走到院门前时，鼹鼠突然一动不动地站住了。

“我看见了一片云！”鼹鼠说。

“只是一小片罢了，”老鼠说，“很快就会散掉的。”

“可能会越聚越大，”鼹鼠说，“也可能是一片雨云呢。我得回去穿上雨衣雨靴、戴上雨帽。”

在等鼹鼠的时候，老鼠忍不住掏了掏篮子，吃了三块奶酪黄瓜三明治。

“我来喽！”鼹鼠终于出来了，“刮风下雨也不怕！”

他们沿着一条小路向前走。走着走着，鼹鼠突然停住脚步。

“那块云团明显变大了，”他对老鼠说，“我还感觉身边刮起了一丝冷风。老鼠啊，说不定会下雪呢，我得回去戴上我的羊绒帽、围巾和手套。”

在等鼹鼠的时候，老鼠忍不住掏了掏篮子，吃了些饼干，喝了点儿酸橙汁。

“我来喽！”鼹鼠终于回来了，“瞧我，外头套羊绒，夹层穿雨衣，贴身的是天晴时穿的衣服——无论什么天气我都准备好了。”

他们继续往前走了一小段路，哪知鼹鼠又站住了。

“我的睡衣裤呢？”鼹鼠说。

“你的睡衣裤怎么了？”老鼠问。

“这次野餐可能会走得很远，来不及赶回家睡觉。”鼹鼠说，“我得回去拿上睡衣裤，以防万一。”

在等鼹鼠的时候，老鼠忍不住掏了掏篮子，吃了一些薯片、几个糖霜小圆蛋糕和两个苹果。

“我来喽！”鼹鼠终于回来了，“我拿了睡衣裤——你猜怎么着？我还带了游泳的东西。说不定能找到地方下水呢。”

“可是你并不喜欢游泳呀。”老鼠说。

“哦，对啊。”鼹鼠说，“我都忘记了。”

老鼠把沾在胡子上的碎屑掸掉。

“鼹鼠，”他说，“你已经走了很长一段路了吧？”

“嗯？对啊，你这样一说倒提醒了我，”鼹鼠说，“我刚才来来回回走了好几趟呢。”

“这就好。”老鼠说，“因为今天的野餐已经没戏了。”

“为什么呢？”鼹鼠问。

“我呀，已经把篮子里的食物全吃光了。”老鼠说。

“我早就想过，也许会有突发情况。”鼹鼠不慌不忙地说，“所以啊，你猜怎么着？”

“怎么着？”老鼠问。

“我在口袋里另放了一份食物，不如我们就在这儿坐下来吃吧。”

“你自己吃吧，鼹鼠，我已经饱了。我这就去好好走一走。”

于是，老鼠自己出发了。

MOUSE & MOLE

Joyce Dunbar and James Mayhew

Talk to Me

'Talk to me,' said Mouse.

'What about?' said Mole.

'Anything,' said Mouse.

'I can't think of anything,' said Mole. 'Give me some ideas.'

'You could tell me what we are going to do tomorrow,' said Mouse.

'What are we going to do tomorrow?' said Mole.

'Well,' said Mouse. 'If it's a fine day we are going on a picnic in the woods. We are making cheese and cucumber sandwiches and we are taking our new picnic basket with cups and saucers and plates.'

'So we are,' said Mole. 'But what if it isn't a fine day?'

'If it isn't a fine day,' said Mouse, 'we are going to make an apple wood fire. We will sit in our cosy armchairs and roast chestnuts and toast muffins. We will have hot chocolate to drink.'

'So we will,' said Mole. 'But what if it's an in-between sort of day?'

'We will do something in-between,' said Mouse. 'We

will tidy up.'

'So we will,' said Mole.

'Thank you for talking to me,' said Mouse.

'That's all right,' said Mole.

Salad

Mole's snout peeped out of the bedclothes.

'What sort of day is it?' he asked.

'Wild and wintry,' said Mouse.

Mole snuggled his snout back down. 'In that case I'll stay in bed.'

'Don't you worry,' said Mouse. 'I will make an apple wood fire in the sitting room. Then you will want to get up.'

Mouse made an apple wood fire. Mole's snout sniffed apple wood smoke. Soon he was shuffling downstairs.

'How I hate these wild and wintry days,' he grumbled. 'All we can do is huddle by the fire.'

'We can do more than that,' said Mouse. 'We can toast

some muffins. We can roast some chestnuts.'

'Good,' said Mole. 'I'm hungry.'

So Mouse toasted some muffins and roasted some chestnuts.

'Are there any more?' asked Mole when he had eaten a plateful.

'Are there any more?' Mole asked again when he had eaten a second plateful.

'I've eaten too much,' said Mole when he had eaten a third plateful. 'Tomorrow I will eat only salad.'

'That's a good idea,' said Mouse.

'It is,' said Mole. 'So why wait? I will start my diet now. Have we got any salad, Mouse?

'We have,' said Mouse. 'We have carrots and radishes and spinach.'

'Then I'll have some,' said Mole, and he ate a plateful of salad.

'Aren't I good?' he said. 'I have eaten all the salad. I think I deserve a little treat. Butter some muffins, Mouse. Roast a few more of those chestnuts.'

Then Mole ate another plateful. 'Wintry days are not so bad after all,' he said, falling into a snooze.

Tidying Up

'Hurray!' said Mouse the next morning. 'The sun is shining today. Today we can go on our picnic!'

'No we can't,' said Mole. 'I ate too much yesterday. I ate toasted muffins and salad. Then I ate more toasted muffins. Today I will eat nothing at all. I will do exercises instead.'

But when Mole went into the sitting room to do his exercises, he found it was all of a clutter.

'We will have to tidy up, Mouse. I need some space to bend and stretch.'

So Mouse bent down and picked all the clutter up from the floor. Mole collected all the bits and bobs from the shelves. Mouse cleared away all the odds and ends from the sofa. They piled everything into the kitchen.

'There!' said Mouse when they had finished. 'Now there's room for you to bend and stretch!'

'But what about my deep breathing?' said Mole. 'I need fresh air for deep breathing. Here there is too much dust. We will have to dust and sweep, Mouse.'

So Mouse got down on his four paws and swept the

floor. Mole stretched on tiptoe to dust the cobwebs off the ceiling and shelves. They worked so hard that soon they were out of breath.

'Phew!' panted Mouse when they had finished. 'I'm puffed. But now you can do your exercises.'

'Exercises!' said Mole. 'I'm too exhausted to exercise! What I need is a cup of tea. Come on, Mouse. Follow me into the kitchen. We deserve a cup of tea.'

But when they went into the kitchen to make a cup of tea, they found it was all of a clutter.

'Mouse,' said Mole. 'We will have to tidy up. There's no room to make a cup of tea.'

So together they tidied up the kitchen. They scooped up all the bits and bobs. They gathered in all the odds and ends. They bundled them into the bedroom. It took them the rest of the day.

'There!' said Mole when they had finished. 'We've tidied up the sitting room. We've tidied up the kitchen. We deserve a cup of tea and something to eat as well. How about pancakes and treacle?'

So Mouse made a pile of pancakes while Mole got out a tin of treacle.

'I need an early night after that,' said Mole when he

had finished.

'So do I,' said Mouse.

But when they went into the bedroom for their early night, they found it was all of a clutter.

'Mouse,' said Mole. 'Just look at my bed. It is covered with odds and ends.'

'And just look at mine,' said Mouse. 'It is piled with bits and bobs.'

They flopped into bed just the same. They were much too tired to care...

Stuff

'Help!' cried Mole the next morning. 'I am being buried alive.'

'I know just how you feel,' said Mouse. 'Come on. We will have to tidy up.'

'But we tidied up yesterday,' said Mole.

'We did. But we did it all wrong,' said Mouse.

'The problem, you see, is stuff. We've got too much

stuff. We didn't tidy it up at all. We moved it from room to room. We need to get rid of it altogether.'

'But I like stuff,' said Mole. 'Stuff is very interesting. It might come in useful one day.'

'You can have stuff, or you can have space,' said Mouse. 'But you can't have both.'

'But what is the use of space if you have no stuff to put in it?' asked Mole.

'Space is space,' said Mouse, 'and stuff is stuff. Come on. Let's take some stuff to the rubbish dump and we can have some space for a change. Help me to fill these sacks.'

Together they filled three sacks.

'You are right, Mouse,' said Mole when they had finished. 'Look at all this lovely space. No more tidying up! No more stuff to tidy!'

'We can take these sacks on the motorbike,' said Mouse.

'Whose turn is it to drive?'

'Mine,' said Mole. 'Same as last time.'

There were three big skips at the rubbish dump. One was marked 'Glass'. Another was marked 'Paper'. A third was marked 'Metal'.

Mouse threw all the newspapers into the skip marked 'Paper'. 'That's that!' he said.

'But look at that bundle of comics,' said Mole. 'They look very interesting. I must take them home.'

And he filled up the sack with old comics.

Then Mouse threw all the empty jars and bottles into the skip marked 'Glass'. 'That's that!' he said.

'But look at that old mirror,' said Mole, 'and that fish tank. I must take them home. You never know, they might come in useful.'

And he put them into a sack.

Mouse threw all the old tin cans and old pans into the skip marked 'Metal'. 'That's that!' he said.

'But look at those coat hangers, and that old tin trunk, and those metal springs. I must take them home. They might come in useful,' said Mole.

And he filled up the last of the sacks.

So Mole and Mouse rode home, carrying three sacks full of stuff.

'How clever you are to think of making all that space,' said Mole. 'Now we have somewhere to put all this stuff.'

He tipped the comics on to the sofa in the sitting room. He put the fish tank and the mirror on the shelves. He

emptied the coat hangers and the tin trunk and the metal springs onto the floor. There was no room left for Mouse and Mole.

Mouse scratched his head.

'As I was saying, Mole, you can have stuff, or you can have space, but you can't have both. We will have to stay outside.'

Mouse sat down on the steps. Mole twiddled a broken spring. 'I brought this one specially for you,' said Mole. But Mouse wasn't pleased. Not a bit!

The Picnic

'I think we should go on our picnic today,' said Mouse. 'I feel like a good long walk.'

'So do I,' said Mole. 'But what about the weather?'

'It's fine,' said Mouse. 'The sun is shining and there's hardly a cloud in the sky.'

'In that case I shall wear my T-shirt and shorts and sun hat,' said Mole.

'And I will pack the hamper,' said Mouse.

Soon they were ready to go. They had just reached the gate when Mole suddenly stopped stock-still.

'I can see a cloud!' he said.

'It's only a little cloud,' said Mouse. 'It will soon go away.'

'It might get bigger,' said Mole. 'It might be a rain cloud. I must put on my mackintosh and galoshes and sou'wester.'

While Mouse was waiting for Mole, he couldn't resist a little dip into the hamper. He ate three of the cheese and cucumber sandwiches.

'Here I am!' said Mole at last. 'Ready to face the rain!'

They had walked along a little way when Mole stopped in his tracks.

'That cloud is definitely getting bigger,' he said to Mouse, 'and I can feel a chill wind getting up. You never know, Mouse, it might snow. I must go back for my woolly hat and scarf and mittens.'

While Mouse waited for Mole, he couldn't resist a little dip into the hamper. He had some biscuits and some lime juice cordial.

'Here I am!' said Mole at last. 'Ready to face any

weather! I have my woolly things on top, and my rain things underneath, and my sun things underneath that.'

They had walked a little way further when Mole stopped still once more.

'What about my pyjamas?' he said.

'What about your pyjamas?' asked Mouse.

'We might walk so far on our picnic that we might not get back in time for bed,' said Mole. 'I must go back for my pyjamas just in case.'

While Mouse waited for Mole, he couldn't resist a little dip into the hamper. He ate some crisps, some iced buns and two apples.

'Here I am!' said Mole at last. 'I've got my pyjamas. And guess what? I have remembered my swimming things as well. You never know, we might find a place to swim.'

'But you don't like swimming,' said Mouse.

'So I don't,' said Mole. 'I forgot.'

Mouse brushed some crumbs from his whiskers.

'Mole,' he said. 'Have you had a good long walk?'

'Why, yes I have, come to think of it,' said Mole. 'With all that to-ing and fro-ing.'

'Good,' said Mouse, 'because we are not going on a

picnic after all.'

'Why not?' said Mole.

'Because I have eaten all the food in the hamper,' said Mouse.

'I thought there might be an emergency,' said Mole, 'so guess what?'

'What?' said Mouse.

'I have packed another picnic in my pockets. Why don't we sit down right here and eat it?'

'You can eat it, Mole. I'm full up. I'm going for a good long walk.'

And Mouse did.

Raffle Ticket No7
10p
Woodside Dry Cleaners. receipt for Jacket and bow tie.
Mouse
STAMFORD, LINCS.
Dear Mouse
Weather fine and sunny. Have been Picnicing on common. Love Rat.
Mr. Mouse
The woods
(Just past Rabbits hole)

your sight
test is on 7.3.82
at 2.30pm
Mole
you are cordially invited to Rabbits birthday party.
Bring a cake. R.S.V.P.
SCUNTHORPE-ON-SEA
Having a lovely time, wish you were here!
from Rabbit.
To Mole esq.
The Woods
(Near Owls tree)
(Don't know Postcode)
MoLe
To be kept